LONG
DISTANCE

Also by Whitney Gardner

Fake Blood

Becoming RBG

LONG DISTANCE

WHITNEY GARDNER

SIMON & SCHUSTER BOOKS FOR YOUNG READERS

NEW YORK   LONDON   TORONTO   SYDNEY   NEW DELHI

SIMON & SCHUSTER BOOKS FOR YOUNG READERS

An imprint of Simon & Schuster Children's Publishing Division

1230 Avenue of the Americas, New York, New York 10020

SIMON & SCHUSTER BOOKS FOR YOUNG READERS

and related marks are trademarks of Simon & Schuster, Inc.

For information about special discounts for bulk purchases, please contact Simon & Schuster Special Sales at 1-866-506-1949 or business@simonandschuster.com.

The Simon & Schuster Speakers Bureau can bring authors to your live event. For more information or to book an event, contact the Simon & Schuster Speakers Bureau at 1-866-248-3049 or visit our website at www.simonspeakers.com.

Also available in a Simon & Schuster Books for Young Readers hardcover edition

Interior design by Tom Daly

The text for this book was set in Minion, WGH2, and WGH3.

The illustrations for this book were rendered digitally.

Manufactured in China

0421 SCP

First Simon & Schuster Books for Young Readers paperback edition June 2021

2 4 6 8 10 9 7 5 3 1

Library of Congress Cataloging-in-Publication Data

Names: Gardner, Whitney, author, illustrator.

Title: Long distance / Whitney Gardner.

Description: First edition. | New York : Simon & Schuster Books for Young Readers, [2021] | Audience: Ages 10 up. | Audience: Grades 4–6. | Summary: After moving to Seattle, Vega's dads send her to the very strange Camp Best Friend, where she discovers that one can make new friends without forgetting old ones.

Identifiers: LCCN 2020010343 (print) | LCCN 2020010344 (eBook) | ISBN 9781534455665 (hardcover) | ISBN 9781534455658 (paperback) | ISBN 9781534455672 (eBook)

Subjects: CYAC: Friendship—Fiction. | Camps—Fiction. | Moving, Household—Fiction. | Family life—Fiction. | Gay fathers—Fiction. | Science fiction.

Classification: LCC PZ7.1.G373 Lon 2021 (print) | LCC PZ7.1.G373 (eBook) | DDC [Fic]—dc23

LC record available at https://lccn.loc.gov/2020010343

LC ebook record available at https://lccn.loc.gov/2020010344

To all my friends both
near and far, far away

CHAPTER 1
Start small with people you know.

LONG
DISTANCE

A WEEK LATER IN VEGA'S NEW SEATTLE BEDROOM.

Look! I actually have a good window for my telescope here.

Ooh, which direction?

Northern facing, see?

Lotsa light pollution, though.

20

MAKE YOUR NEXT FRIEND AT CAMP VERY BEST FRIEND.

PARTICIPATE IN DOZENS OF FUN ACTIVITES WITH YOUR **NEW FRIEND.**

ENJOY SPECIAL FIRESIDE TREATS AND STORIES WITH YOUR **NEW FRIEND!**

VBF

YOUR **NEW BEST FRIEND** AWAITS YOU UNDER THE STARS!

CAMP VERY BEST FRIEND, FOR THE BEST OF FRIENDS.

I'm ready when you are.

I wish you would stop saying that. Camp won't be an adventure. Moving here wasn't. It's just a thing we had to do— that you wanted us to do.

Hmm. I'm sorry if it feels that way.

It's not the worst thing. It's just not an adventure. It's just... I dunno. Different.

I know it's very different and new. It could end up being fun. What's the harm in trying?

Because it's weird! To just assume some stranger is going to like you.

TIPS FOR MAKING FRIENDS:

1. Start small with people you know.

2. Get yourself out there.

3. Take the first step.

4. Be open.

5. Get to know the person.

6. Be there for them.

7. Make the effort.

46

CHAPTER 3
Take the first step.

WHAT ARE THUNDER EGGS?

Thunder eggs are round rock-like formations that start with hollow centers.

Over thousands of years, small fractures in the rock let mineral-laced waters seep into the void, and these waters form the new core of the rock.

With the appearance of a rough rock on the outside, a cut and polish will reveal the core of beautiful mineral deposits.

Does this one look like a thunder egg, Gemma?!

Nah. Too small.

We'll find one eventually.

Just gotta keep digging.

89

93

Does that seem heavy to you?

It sure felt heavy.

You didn't have to leave the group. I wasn't going to get lost. I have an excellent sense of direction. I think.

I'm sorry about *Mr. President* back there. I don't know why all the counselors are obsessed with him.

Eh, I'm pretty used to it. I don't normally let that stuff get to me, but...

Hey Halley,
So it's official. This camp is weird. I wish my parents had let me stay home. How am I going to get through two whole weeks out here? And all alone?

How's Portland? Are you racing in the soapbox derby again this year?

My phone doesn't work at all out here. I'm glad I remembered to pack some stamps. Sorry if you've been trying to reach me.

I've been trying to talk to you. What happened? It's okay. I know long distance is hard. Should it be this hard? Just... what happened? Did you make new friends already? I'm sorry if I said something dumb.

Write back soon?
Vega

EARTH Day
FOREVER USA

106

It's a little speaker, look.

No. Way.

1. The sat phone sends out a signal that passes into the speaker through a magnet.

3. The diaphragm passes on these vibrations to the surrounding air, which makes the noise!

2. The current from the signal flows through a wire coil and generates a magnetic field around it. This causes the wire and diaphragm to vibrate.

So I collected a bunch more today and every single one is the same. Even if they look different on the outside, they're all metal on the inside.

Gemma, show them what else you found. Might as well.

Look. I'm not trying to get all buddy-buddy with you guys... but if something bad is happening I guess you should know.

Look, I'm just telling you what I think. And what I know. And what I figured out all on my own, so...

What if we really *are* being watched?

By who? The Eye? Bigfoot?

More like a clandestine government agency hiding microphones in the trees and stuff.

Why would they spy on kids making arts and crafts?

And these are speakers,

Microphones and speakers are almost interchangeable, right?

Vega! You're going with HIS idea?

147

Why won't the needle move?
Is it stuck? Did I break it?

Those clouds might make this difficult.

A sextant is a device used for celestial navigation. It measures the angle between two objects by using mirrors.

INDEX MIRROR

HORIZON MIRROR

EYEPIECE

GRADUATED ARC

INDEX ARM

The horizon mirror is semi-transparent so you can see the horizon through it.

The index mirror is attached to a movable arm. This mirror will reflect the light from the sun or other stars back to the horizon mirror.

The index arm moves so the image of the sun can align with the horizon in the reflection.

The angle between the sun and horizon can be read off of the graduated arc to help calculate your location.

The sextant helps sailors navigate while at sea, and has been used for hundreds of years! Unfortunately for Vega...

I'm not near the ocean. I can't even see Puget Sound.

CHAPTER 5
Get to know them.

229

CHAPTER 7

Make the effort.

297

Well, I knew something was wrong because I couldn't get in touch with you. And when I called your dads they said they hadn't heard from you either.

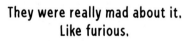

They were really mad about it. Like furious.

Yeah, like that!